Contents

Chapter 1
Tall and Small

Frankie was head and shoulders above everyone else in his class. He was thin and he was tall.

"Lanky Frankie!" That's what some people in his class called him.

"Beanpole!" That's what some of the others called him.

The rest of the class would make pretend binoculars with their hands. They would look up and stare at Frankie as if his head was as far away as the moon.

The only person who didn't make fun of Frankie was Molly. Molly was so short she was head and shoulders below everyone else.

Guess what most of the class called her? Mini-Molly.

Guess what the rest of the class called her? Molly the Dolly.

Sometimes they made pretend binoculars with their hands. They stared down at Molly as if she was as far away as Australia.

The only person who didn't make fun of Molly was Frankie.

Frankie had no idea why the other children in his class were so unkind. Frankie didn't call

them names. He didn't pretend they were so small he needed binoculars to see them. He only wanted to be friends. Why did everyone have to make a stupid fuss and make Frankie feel like such a freak?

Frankie kept his thoughts to himself. But Molly didn't. She had no idea why the class behaved like this either, so she shouted back at everyone.

"My name is NOT Mini-Molly, stinky-pants!" she would shout.

Or she might yell, "I am NOT called Molly the Dolly, you wally!"

But no matter what Molly and Frankie did, it didn't stop the rest of the class making fun of them. They laughed when Frankie was silent and they laughed if Molly answered them back.

When Frankie went home at the end of each day he felt as miserable as a wet weekend.

When Molly went home she felt angry enough to burst.

Frankie and Molly were not exactly friends. Frankie didn't think it was a good idea to be friends with a girl. But Molly didn't think it mattered who you were friends with. She'd be quite happy to be friends with a boy – or a chimpanzee for that matter. But she didn't have a chimpanzee. So she had to make do with Frankie, even though she thought Frankie was very tall – and silly.

Sometimes Molly and Frankie would walk home together. Frankie seemed to have a sad grey cloud hovering over his high-in-the-sky head. It was raining from his cloud. Molly seemed to have a storm cloud hovering over her not-far-off-the-ground head. Lightning stabbed from her cloud.

Chapter 2
A Big Idea

You might think that Frankie's dad would be very tall. You might even think that Frankie's mum would be very tall. They weren't. They were both a normal size. In fact, Frankie was already much taller than them.

But Frankie's mum and dad's height was just about the only normal thing about them. They collected elephants.

Some of the elephants were carved from wood or made from clay. Some were pictures on cushions. Some were stuffed and fluffy. They came in all sizes, and there were hundreds of them. The biggest one was in the garden. When Frankie was a baby he used its trunk as a slide. But Frankie wasn't a baby any more. In fact, he was now so tall he was longer than the elephant's trunk.

The smallest elephant was in the bathroom. Its body was made of blue rubber. Its head had pink ears that stuck out and a green trunk with a hole at the end. When Frankie had a bath, he would fill the smallest elephant with water and squeeze it hard. Water would shoot out of its trunk. Frankie liked to imagine he was riding a real elephant that was squirting the whole of his class at school. Only Molly had a big umbrella and wellies to protect her.

Frankie's parents could see that Frankie was not very happy at school. They were pretty sure they knew why and they came up with lots of ways to help him.

"Try not to listen to what they say," his mum said. "They're just trying to wind you up."

Frankie knew she was only trying to help, but what was he supposed to do? Stuff his ears with cheese?

Frankie's dad had a different idea. "When they call you names, why don't you try whistling a good, loud tune?" he said. "That would show them that you don't care."

"Nice try, Dad," Frankie said. "But I don't know how to whistle."

"How about singing, then?" his dad said.

"OK," Frankie said. "I'll give it a go."

At school the next day, Jordan called Frankie a string bean.

Frankie opened his mouth and sang at the top of his voice. "Old MacDonald had a farm, ee-i, ee-i, o!" It was the first song that came into his head.

"He's gone mad!" Jordan laughed. "Hey, everyone! We've got a mad string bean in class."

"There were ten green bottles hanging on the wall," Frankie sang. He was clutching at straws.

"Lanky Frankie's gone all cranky!" the class yelled. Then they laughed even more.

Frankie went home more miserable than ever. "It didn't work," he told his parents. "I sounded like a two-year-old at a nursery sing-along."

"Never mind, Frankie," his mum said. "Your father and I have got another brilliant idea."

"It's a biggie!" His dad grinned. "It's a whopper! It's a tip-top topper!"

Frankie's mum smiled at him. "How do you fancy going to a new school?"

Frankie frowned and shook his head. "How would that make any difference?" he asked. "I'll still be tall. Everyone there will make fun of me too."

"No they won't," his mum said. "This is a very special kind of school. It's called Monster School."

Monster School? Frankie wasn't sure if he liked the sound of that. A school for monsters? Did that mean his mum and dad thought he was a monster? No, no, no!

"I'm not a monster," he whispered. He wanted to yell really, REALLY loudly that he wasn't a monster, but he didn't. If he shouted

like that he would sound just like a monster, wouldn't he?

Frankie's father smiled and put his arm around Frankie.

"Of course you're not a monster," he said. "That's the whole point. Monster School is definitely NOT a school for monsters. In fact, the monsters are –"

Dad stopped and smiled at Frankie.

"Well," Dad went on. "Let's just say it's a school where they give you some very special lessons. Then, when you are ready, you go back to ordinary school. Nobody will tease you again because you'll know just how to deal with them."

"That's right," Mum said. "And another thing you might like is that there is no Monster School on Mondays."

12

Frankie's eyes boggled. No school on Mondays? Hooray! "But isn't that a bit weird?" he said.

"Yes," Mum said. "I know it's strange, but the teachers told us they need Mondays off to recover from the weekend."

For a few moments Frankie wondered what on earth the teachers did at the weekend that was so tiring, but then he forgot about that. He was going to a new school! Mondays off! Fantastic!

A small smile crept onto Frankie's face. It was the first time his parents had seen him smile for months. Frankie was feeling hopeful at last. On Monday – no, on Tuesday! – he was going to go to Monster School and learn how to deal with his class-mates. That seemed like a very, very good idea.

Chapter 3
Monster School?

Monster School didn't look like a special school. It looked like a perfectly ordinary school. The children there looked quite normal. The only difference from Frankie's old school was that these children didn't start the day by calling him names. In fact, they all looked a bit like Frankie – worried.

Frankie had a shock when the teacher walked into the classroom. She had black hair, a black dress, and a black cape with scarlet lining. Her face was chalk-white, apart from her lips, which were blood-red. She had hypnotic green eyes. His teacher was a vampire!

"My name is Miss Stake," she hissed, and the class giggled. "Put up your hand if you think my name is funny," Miss Stake ordered.

One boy raised his hand. Oh dear! That was a mistake. Miss Stake bent over his table.

"Tell me what you see," she ordered.

All of a sudden, she threw open her mouth to reveal four needle-sharp fangs. There were traces of blood on them. The boy almost fainted. Miss Stake laughed.

"The blood on my fangs comes from the last child that thought my name was funny," she said. "Now then, what are you going to say, you horrid little creature?"

"Sorry, sorry, sorry, sorry, sorry," went the boy, staring at a drop of blood on his table.

"Good," Miss Stake said. "The rest of you, be warned. I have very little patience today. I am very tired after a busy weekend. Oh! The necks I had to bite! It takes an awful lot out of a person to suck blood. Not many people know that."

The children listened rather nervously and then the lesson began.

"I am here to teach you how to be a vampire," Miss Stake told them. "Open that trunk at the back of the class."

The trunk was full of vampire costumes. Frankie was sure none of them would be long enough to fit him, because nothing ever was. But one of the outfits was a perfect fit.

"Frankie," Miss Stake said, "you can give out the teeth. These are blunt ones to begin with. When you get older and better at being vampires you might like to get your own nice sharp ones, like mine."

Frankie went round the class, handing out the fangs to everyone. Then they spent the morning learning how to be vampires.

They tried biting each other's necks. They tried swirling their capes. They practised the vampire laugh, which is a lot more difficult than it sounds. They tried talking like vampires too. They said things like –

"I have you in my power!"

"Soon you will join the un-dead!"

"Now I shall drain every drop of blood from your body!"

By the end of the day, Frankie's head was full of swirling capes and his teeth hurt. He flew all the way home like a blood-thirsty bat.

When Frankie got in, his mother asked him if he'd had a good day.

"Now I shall drain every drop of blood from your body!" Frankie growled.

His mother fainted on the spot. Frankie didn't have his costume on. He didn't even have his blunt fangs in. He was rather pleased with himself. He felt rather like a real vampire.

Chapter 4
Lessons

On Wednesday, the children had a new teacher.

It wasn't Miss Stake. It was a dog – a very big, grey, furry dog. With one leap, the dog leaped up onto the teacher's desk. It looked into the eyes of each child in class in turn. Its own eyes flickered like golden flames.

"My name is Wild One," the beast announced. "Before you call me a dog, beware. Wolves are not like Labradors and Alsatians and Poodles. Wolves are the only true dogs. But today, my children, you are not going to learn how to be a wolf. You will learn something of far greater power. I shall teach you how to be – a werewolf. Awhoooooooooo!"

Wild One's howl made Frankie's blood turn to ice-cubes in his veins. It was the most scary noise he had ever heard. But five minutes later, Frankie found himself trying to make the exact same noise. Wild One was teaching the class how to howl like a werewolf.

"Awhoooooooooooo!" the whole class howled.

Wild One sat on the desk and scratched himself under the chin. "Pathetic," he growled. "That wouldn't scare an ant. Try again."

"Awhooooooooooooooooooooo!"

Wild One slumped across his desk. "I'm going to sleep," he told them. "Go outside and practise. Don't come back until you can scare the pants off each other."

It took a lot of hard work, but at last the class managed it. They went back to the classroom and showed Wild One their terrified pants.

"I don't believe those pants have been scared off you," Wild One told the class. "Howl once more – and make it fierce."

"AWHOOOOOOO!" went the whole class.

Wild One's fur stood on end. He grinned and showed all his glittering teeth. "Well done," he said. "Top marks. Now I shall teach you how to turn into a werewolf."

This was much harder work. It needed to be done in secret. Wild One went to each child and whispered magic into their ear. One by one, the children turned into werewolves. Hair grew on their hands and faces. Ears turned

pointy. Teeth grew long and sharp. Tongues flopped out of their mouths.

The class looked at each other and laughed at their new bodies.

"Look at me! I'm so hairy!" said Niko, the boy who had almost fainted on the first day.

"Hairy-scary," Frankie grinned.

In their final lesson that day, the class learned how to run like the wind. They learned how to leap over hedges and walls as if they were no obstacle at all.

By the end of the day, Frankie was still bouncing with energy and tingling all over. He galloped home with his tongue flopping out his mouth and his nose sniff-sniffing every lamp-post.

When he got home, his dad asked him if he'd had a good day.

"Awhooooooooo!" Frankie howled. His dad fainted on the spot.

Frankie grinned. He scratched himself under his chin for ages. Then he went to bed.

Chapter 5
Take Off Your Head

Thursday came. Frankie sat in class and wondered what kind of teacher they would have today. He was getting used to this strange school. He was not all that surprised when the classroom door opened and a man with no head walked in.

That's not true. The new teacher did have a head, but he was carrying it under his arm.

"I am Sir Headless Ghost," the teacher told the class. "And that is what I am – a headless ghost. Today you will learn how to take off your head and carry it under your arm. It's not as easy as it sounds."

Frankie thought it didn't sound easy at all. He had a question to ask, an important question. He waved his hand in the air until the teacher noticed him.

"Yes, young Frankie?" said Sir Headless Ghost.

"Please, Sir Headless," Frankie said. "If we take off our heads, won't all the blood spurt out of our necks until we die?"

"That is an excellent, sensible question," said Sir Headless. "That is why you need this lesson. Today I will teach you how to take off your head without loss of blood. After all, if the whole class died in my lesson I wouldn't have any pupils left. Besides, it is just possible that your parents might complain."

Frankie tried not to chuckle. He decided he liked Sir Headless.

Soon the class were learning Stage 1 of Head Removal. Sir Headless called this a breathing exercise, but as far as Frankie could tell it was just holding your breath for as long as possible.

Then came Stage 2 of Head Removal. This was called Plop the Plug.

"Imagine you are holding a very large, heavy rubber bath plug in your right hand," Sir Headless said. "Then hold your breath. With a fast double-reverse twist and spin, remove your head with your left hand and plop the plug back in place on your neck. The plug will stop all your blood spurting out."

"But the plug isn't real," said Pippa, one of Frankie's new class-mates. "It's imaginary."

"In that case, make sure it's only imaginary blood coming out," Sir Headless said. Everyone laughed, even Pippa.

Stage 3 of Head Removal was all about learning how to walk with your head under your arm instead of in its usual place.

"One of the great things about not having your head on your neck is that you can see round things," Sir Headless told the class. He held his head in both hands and shoved it round a corner of the desk. "Or you can lift your head up high to see over things, or turn it round to see behind you."

"That is so brilliant," Niko sighed.

"Yes. I thought you might like that one." Sir Headless smiled. "Now we come to the most difficult part of this class. If you can do this,

you will be top-notch Head Removal experts. This is a trick that I use at the Horror Hotel where I work every weekend. It's hard work, but I just love to see guests faint all over the place," Sir Headless told them.

"This is what you do," he said. "Take off your head and put it on your table. Walk to the end of the room and then back to the table. Now replace your head on your shoulders."

This caused chaos. As the class wandered about headless, they banged into each other and tripped over everything, including themselves. They couldn't see where they were going. Frankie, Niko and Pippa were the only ones who could do it properly.

"Well done!" Sir Headless cried. "You three are my star pupils."

At the end of the day, Frankie was so tired that he thought his head would fall off all by itself. When he got home his parents were already in bed.

"We thought we'd lie down before you showed us what you learned today," Dad told Frankie. He had a nervous look in his eye.

"It's fine," Frankie told them.

"Right." Mum nodded. She settled back on her pillow. "You can show us now."

"OK. There's no need to lose your heads," Frankie said. He placed his hands on his head. "Because I'm going to lose mine!"

And Frankie took off his head and tucked it under his arm.

"Oh my giddy aunt," Mum said.

This time, both his parents fainted. Frankie was beginning to think that maybe he should learn some First Aid.

Chapter 6
A Spooky Spook

It was Friday and it was Frankie's last day at
Monster School. He sat in class and waited for
the door to open. It didn't. That was because
the teacher came in through the wall instead.

"My name is Miss Shadow," she said. "As
you can all see, I am a spooky spook. Today is
your last day. I am going to teach you how to
appear beside someone all of a sudden so that
you can tap them on the shoulder and go BOO!

If you behave yourselves, I shall also teach you how to pass through walls."

Frankie thought that both these tricks could be very useful. Sadly, Miss Shadow was not a very good teacher. She kept vanishing. Then she would appear again somewhere quite different. She also had a habit of appearing next to you when you didn't want her to.

When Frankie went to the toilet, Miss Shadow drifted in through the cubicle walls.

"Oh there you are, Frankie," she said. "Hurry up, now."

Frankie decided that this was one trick he didn't like very much – when it was played on him.

But by the afternoon most of the class were getting very good at creeping up on each other. Next, Miss Shadow gave them a special lesson on how to say "BOO!" and make people jump out of their skin.

"It's not good to shout BOO!" she told them. "It's the way you say it that's important. Try to sound like a spooky spook – a quiet whisper often works best. I do this a lot at weekends when I work at the Horror Hotel with Sir Headless Ghost. I creep up ever so quietly and whisper in a guest's ear. You should see them jump! And the screams! Hilarious!"

"Boo!" the class whispered like spooky spooks, and they all jumped out of their skins.

"How UTTERLY shocking." Miss Shadow smiled. She had turned even paler than usual. "You may go home now," she said. "Frankie, you stay behind, please. I would like a word with you."

The rest of the class slid through the walls and out into the playground.

Frankie went across to the teacher's desk. Miss Shadow glided round and eyed him carefully.

"Frankie, the other teachers have told me that you have been very good in class, and that you have listened well and worked hard. In fact, you are our star pupil. You are top of the class."

"Thank you." Frankie beamed. He had never been top of anything before, apart from being the tallest in his old class, which was not at all the same kind of thing.

"But there is one final lesson you still have to learn," Miss Shadow warned.

"What's that?" Frankie asked.

"I'm afraid I can't tell you," Miss Shadow said. "You will only know the answer when you know the answer."

"But that makes no sense," Frankie said with a frown.

Miss Shadow smiled at him. "Maybe it doesn't, but it's true. When you learn your final lesson you will understand what I mean."

Frankie left school feeling cross. He didn't like riddles. But he did like being top of the class. When he got home, his parents were in bed again. This time, they were hiding under the sheets.

"We don't want to know what you did today," they shouted. "It's all far too scary for us."

"I promise not to show you," Frankie said with a grin. "But I did come top of the class."

So his parents came out from under the sheets and Dad ordered take-away pizzas to celebrate.

"It's back to your old school on Monday," Mum said.

"Oh, good!" said Frankie. It was time to stop his old class-mates poking fun at him – and at Molly.

Chapter 7
Show and Tell Time

"Look!" everyone shouted in the school playground on Monday morning. "Lanky Frankie is back!"

The children all crowded round him.

"Where have you been, Frankie?" Sasha asked. "Did someone think you were a bean pole and stick you in their garden?"

"No, no," Dexter laughed. "They thought he was a tent pole and they took him camping. He spent all night holding up their tent!"

Frankie looked at them all. He wondered what he should do. Should he be a vampire, a werewolf, a headless ghost or a spook? He'd quite like to be all of them. It was Show and Tell time!

First of all, Frankie pulled off his head. He didn't tuck it under his arm. Instead he held it on one hand above his neck, so that he was taller than ever.

"AAAARGH!" the children screamed, and they ran off to the far side of the playground.

Then Frankie put his head back on and after a few moments the children came back across the playground. They could hardly believe their eyes. Had Frankie really taken off his head? Yuk!

But as the children returned, hairs began to grow all over Frankie's face and hands. His teeth became long and sharp. His tongue flopped out of his mouth.

"That's quite clever," Dexter said.

Frankie threw back his head and howled. "Awhoooooooooooooooooooooo!"

"AAAAAAAAAAAARRGGH!" the children screamed, and off they ran again. Dexter ran too. He ran faster than anyone.

Bit by bit, Frankie changed back to his normal self. After a few minutes, everyone crept back towards him.

But before they could get close, there was a puff of smoke and Frankie changed into a vampire. He opened his mouth wide and his fangs dripped blood. And then he laughed the vampire laugh.

"Wa-ha-ha-ha-ha-ha-rarrgh!"

This time nobody screamed. They couldn't. They had all fainted. Every single one of them. Dexter had even fainted twice. They lay in a big circle all round Frankie, as if he had blown them out like candles.

Frankie was VERY pleased. He didn't think the class would ever make jokes about him being too tall again. He sat down on a bench and he waited for them to stop being in a faint. Then, maybe, they could all be friends at last.

One by one, his class-mates got to their feet, looking a bit shaky. Frankie smiled cheerfully and waited for them to come over and talk to him. But they didn't. One by one, his class-mates hurried away.

Frankie was gobsmacked. He was alone. Again.

Chapter 8
Tough Talk

Frankie sat on the bench and stared after his class-mates. After a moment, Molly crept over and sat at the far end of the bench. Frankie gave her a weak smile and gazed at her as if to say, "What did I do?"

Molly stole a glance at his teeth to see if they were sharp or tipped with blood. They weren't, so she moved a little closer.

"Where have they gone?" Frankie asked.

"You've scared them off," Molly said. "What did you think would happen? First of all you pull your head off. Then you go all hairy and howl at them. Next you turn into Dracula. That's not the way to make friends."

Frankie was fed up. "Huh!" he said in a sulk. "I didn't want them to make fun of me any more. That's all."

"Well, they won't," Molly said. "They'll probably never dare speak to you again."

"Oh, rats," Frankie said. He stared at the ground and wished it could tell him what to do. His brain felt like it was spinning round and round in circles, so fast that he couldn't find a way out. He wanted to be friends with everyone, but he also wanted to scare the pants off them.

Molly looked at him. She knew how he felt. She knew what it was like to really, really want a friend. She also knew what it was like to be teased and to feel so angry you wanted to explode and hurt someone.

Molly reached across and held Frankie's hand. "I'm your friend," she said.

"Argh!" Frankie cried, and he snatched his hand away. "But you're a girl!"

Molly's eyes narrowed until they looked like the points on the ends of two daggers. She glared at Frankie so hard it was as if she had turned into all his Monster School teachers rolled into one.

"Sometimes," she told him, "I think that boys can be very, very, very stupid! You've just scared everyone away. I'm the only one who wants to be your friend, and you say 'No way' because I'm a GIRL? How stupid can you be?"

"All right," Frankie said, looking sheepish. "You can be my friend. But you mustn't hold my hand."

"Poor little Fwankie," Molly said in a silly voice. "Fwankie doesn't want to hold hands with the girly." She smiled at him. "All right, I won't hold your hand. Now then, listen. I've got an idea. You're going to teach me how to be a werewolf. Can you do that?"

Frankie thought he could. They went into a dark corner of the playground and he showed Molly all that Wild One had taught him. Molly listened and practised hard. After a while, she got the hang of it. Her hands went a bit hairy. And so did her face.

"Urgh!" she gasped. "I've got a moustache – and a BEARD!"

Molly tried to make her teeth grow, but sadly they fell right out. Then Molly had another go and this time it worked.

Soon Molly was almost as good as Frankie. They both lifted their heads to the moon, opened their mouths and howled.

"Awhoooooooo!"

"Great," said Molly. "Now you wait here, and soon you will have a load of new friends. And not all of them will be girls, don't worry."

Frankie gave a weak smile and watched Molly run off. Then he sat down on the bench again. His class had gone. Molly had gone. He waited, and he waited. Molly had been gone an awfully long time. What was she up to? Doubts crept into Frankie's mind. After a while, he heard a distant howl.

"Awhooooooo!"

Frankie knew it was Molly, as a werewolf.

"Awhooooo! Awhoooooooo!" The cries came again and again.

"Oh great," Frankie said to himself. "Now she's gone and scared them all away again.

What a clever plan that was. What a clever girl. Huh!"

Frankie put his head in his hands and sulked more than ever.

Chapter 9
The Answer

A strange shuffling noise made Frankie sit up straight. He stared across the playground. A crowd of children was approaching. There, right at the front, was Molly. Maybe she hadn't scared everyone away, after all.

On the other hand, maybe they were all coming to laugh at Frankie. Yes, that was it! They were all going to pretend to be werewolves and laugh at him. Well, he didn't care. He still had one trick up his sleeve. He would be a spooky spook and he would creep up on them one by one and scare the pants off them.

The children crept closer and closer. Molly was smiling. Huh! This was the girl who said they could be friends. Double huh huh! This was the girl who had tricked him into teaching her how to be a werewolf. Triple huh huh huh!

Frankie stayed on his bench and glared back at Molly and the class as they all gathered round him.

"Are you ready?" asked Molly. The whole class nodded. "After three," said Molly. "One, two, three –"

"AWHOOOOOOOOOOOOOOOOOOOOOO!"

Frankie's hair stood on end and he fell off his bench.

The class ran up to him and helped him to his feet.

"Are you all right, Frankie?" Dexter asked. "Not too scared? That was such a brilliant trick you taught Molly. She showed us how to do it and now we can be werewolves too."

"Yeah," Sasha shouted. "And we want to know how to pull our heads off! Can you teach us, Frankie? You're amazing. We want to do what you can do."

Soon everyone could do all the things that Frankie had learned at Monster School. But nobody could do them as well as Frankie could. He wasn't just the tallest in the class, he was TOP of the class!

And when the children went off for assembly, they had even more fun. They sat in the hall with their heads under their arms. Miss Pringle, who played the piano while they sang, took one look at them and shrieked. She ran all the way home and hid in her broom cupboard for a week.

After assembly, Mr Powerpump, the games teacher, told the class to get changed for PE. So the children got changed – they changed into werewolves and went "Awhoooooooo!"

Poor Mr Powerpump. He was so scared he scrambled up to the top of the climbing frame and stayed there, chattering like a monkey. He took off his trainers and threw them at the hairy-scary werewolves, but they just gobbled them up – even though they were rather pongy.

At last, Monday came to an end and everyone could go home. (Apart from Miss Pringle, who had already gone home to hide in her broom cupboard. And Mr Powerpump, who was still at the top of the climbing frame without any trainers on.)

Frankie and Molly walked home together. Frankie didn't even notice that Molly was holding his hand.

"What a brilliant day!" Frankie shouted. "I am happy as a headless ghost with two heads!"

"It was brilliant because of YOU," Molly said.

"No, it was brilliant because of YOU," Frankie said. "We've made loads of new friends." Then he noticed they were holding hands. "Oh!" he said.

Molly pulled her hand away. "Never mind," she sighed. "One step at a time. See you at school tomorrow." She skipped off down the road.

When Frankie got home, he was still beaming.

"Wow!" said his dad. "Looks like you've had a tip-top day. What did you do?"

"I was a headless ghost and a werewolf and a vampire," Frankie told them.

"What do you like being the most?" his mum asked.

"Do you know what?" said Frankie. "I think, most of all, I like being Frankie."

That evening, the whole family celebrated. They didn't have pizza this time. They had double pizza and ice cream with chocolate sauce (but not at the same time). Then Frankie went upstairs and had a long bath.

While Frankie was in the bath he looked at the little rubber elephant. It felt funny, but he wasn't interested in the elephant any more. He wasn't bothered about pretending to squirt everyone at school. Instead, Frankie remembered what Miss Shadow had told him.

"You will only know the answer when you know the answer," she had said.

Now Frankie understood what she meant –
and he reckoned he knew the answer. It was
great fun to be a ghost and a werewolf and
a vampire, but it was a lot better just to be
himself and have lots of friends.

Even so, Frankie decided he might have to
do something about Molly. What had she told
him? "One step at a time?" Frankie thought
that sounded a bit scary, even for a boy who'd
survived a perfectly ordinary week at Monster
School.

More from *Jeremy Strong* ...

Living with Vampires
JEREMY STRONG

Kevin's a bit scared of vampires.

Not scared they'll bite his neck. Or scared they'll drink his blood. He's just a bit scared they'll make a fuss at parents' night.

Vampires – they make *such* uncool parents.

The Ghost in the Bath
JEREMY STRONG

Luke is in a lot of rubble – sorry, trouble.

He hasn't done his history project for Mrs Rubble. The last thing he needs is a ghost in the bath ...

Can Ellie the ghost get Luke out of hot water?

Chuckle Bob's Great Escape

JEREMY STRONG

Chuckle Bob doesn't like the pet shop. He wants to be free! But it's hard for a little monkey to live outside in the rain and cold.

Can Chuckle Bob find a new home? Maybe Jessica and Dan can help ...

Mad Iris

JEREMY STRONG

Mad Iris doesn't like the ostrich farm.

She likes Pudding Lane School much better!

But the men from the ostrich farm are hot on her trail ...

Ross and Katie to the rescue!

www.barringtonstoke.co.uk